Jellybean Books™

HENRY
and the Elephant
A Thomas the Tank Engine Storybook

Based on *The Railway Series* **by**

Illustrated by Owa

Random House 🏠 New York

When the director of the railway, Sir Topham Hatt, gave Thomas the Tank Engine his very own set of coaches, he also gave Thomas a line of his own.

Henry the green engine and Gordon the big blue express engine were lonely when Thomas left the yard to run his Branch Line. They missed him very much.

And now they had more work to do, too. Henry and Gordon had to fetch their coaches themselves—and they didn't like that!

Edward the kind blue engine had to do odd jobs, and so did James the proud red engine. Sir Topham Hatt gave Henry and Gordon new coats of paint to cheer them up, but they still grumbled about the extra work.

"We get no rest, we get no rest," they complained as they clanked around the yard. But the coaches only laughed and called Henry and Gordon lazy.

Then one day a circus came to town! The animals rode in special freight cars and the performers rode in special coaches.

All the engines wanted to push and pull the circus freight cars and coaches into place.

When the circus was ready to go on to the next town, Sir Topham Hatt told James to pull the train. That made the other engines dreadfully jealous.

However, they soon forgot about the circus, as they had plenty of work to do.

One morning Henry was told to take some workers to a tunnel that was blocked.

Henry grumbled as he went to find two freight cars to carry the workers and their tools.

"Pushing freight cars! Pushing freight cars!" Henry muttered.

Henry and the freight cars stopped outside the tunnel. The workers tried to look through it, but it was quite dark. No daylight shone from the other end.

The workers took their tools and went inside the tunnel.

Suddenly, with a shout, they all ran out, looking frightened.

"We went up to the thing that was blocking the tunnel and started to dig— but it grunted and moved!" they said.

"Nonsense," said the foreman.

"It's not nonsense," said the workers. "It's big and alive, and we're *not* going in there again!"

"Well," said the foreman, "I'll send the freight cars into the tunnel, and Henry can push the obstacle out."

Henry hated tunnels, but this was worse—something big and alive was inside.

"*Peep peep peep pip pip!*" he whistled. "I don't want to go in!"

"Neither do I," said his driver, "but we must clear the line."

"Oh, dear! Oh, dear!" puffed Henry as they slowly moved into the darkness.

Bump!
Henry's driver shut off the steam at once.
"Help! Help! We're moving backward!" wailed Henry.
Then, moving slowly out into the daylight, came
Henry...and then the freight cars...

...and last of all, pushing hard and looking rather cross, came a large elephant!

"What do you know!" said the foreman. "It must be the missing elephant from the circus."

Henry's driver put on his brakes, and someone ran to telephone the animal keeper.

The elephant stopped pushing and came toward Henry and the workers. They gave him some sandwiches and cake—so he forgot he was cross and remembered he was hungry!

The elephant drank three buckets of water and was just going to drink another when Henry let off steam.

The elephant jumped. With a *Whoo-oosh* he squirted the water all over Henry by mistake.

Poor Henry!

The animal keeper came, and the workers rode home,
laughing happily at their adventure. But Henry was very upset.

"An elephant pushed me! An elephant whooshed
me!" he grumbled.

Once he was back in the shed, Henry told Gordon and
James all about the elephant.